One day, Mama and Baba were watching their kittens practice their calligraphy. As usual, Sagwa finished writing first.

"I'm all done," said Sagwa. She showed Mama her beautiful scroll. "May I go play now?"

"You did very well, Sagwa," purred Mama. "But before you go play, why don't you help your brother and sister finish their calligraphy?"

"But they always take forever!" exclaimed Sagwa.

"Sagwa! You are not being very helpful," said Mama. "Not everyone is as good as you are at calligraphy. Dongwa and Sheegwa just need practice. And some help from their sister!"

"Oh, all right," said Sagwa.

Sagwa walked over to Dongwa and Sheegwa.

"No, that's not right, Sheegwa," said Sagwa. "You have to make the strokes smooth. Yours are messy!"

She turned to Dongwa.
"And you're using way too much ink,
Dongwa! Do it like this!"

But in her rush to show Dongwa, Sagwa spilled the whole bottle of ink all over his scroll!

"Way to go, Sagwa," grumbled Dongwa. "I've been working on this all morning. Now I have to start over again!"

Sagwa felt bad. "Gee . . . I'm sorry. I was just trying to help."

Suddenly, the kittens heard loud, happy music coming from outside. They rushed over to the window.

"It's a parade!" shouted Dongwa.

"Please, Baba, can we go?" said Sheegwa.

"Well, I think you could all use a little fresh air," said Baba.

The three kittens scampered outside
to follow the parade. A crowd had gathered
around some performers.

"What is it?" asked Sheegwa, who
couldn't see past all the people.

"I think they're acrobats," answered
Sagwa.

"No," said Dongwa excitedly. "They're
cats. Acrobat cats!"

The three kittens made their way through the crowd. They watched as the acrobat cats flew through the air. The crowd cheered. So did Dongwa, Sagwa, and Sheegwa.

"I want to be an acrocat when I grow up," said Sheegwa.

"It's acro*bat*." Dongwa laughed.

"Oops," said Sheegwa.

"It's okay, Sheegwa." Sagwa giggled. "But it would be fun. We could travel all over the world, and people would cheer for us!"

Sagwa decided to try her own somersault. *PLOP!* Sagwa landed with a splat in a muddy puddle.

"Good one, Sagwa." Dongwa laughed. "That's more like an acro-SPLAT!"

By the next day, Dongwa and
Sheegwa were doing somersaults.
But not Sagwa. Every time she tried,
she plopped onto the ground.

"Come on, you guys . . . let's do something else," said Sagwa. "Sheegwa – let's practice our calligraphy."

"Writing? Yuck!" said Sheegwa. "I want to be an acrobat!"

Sagwa tried again.
"Hey, Dongwa, how about
flying that kite we painted
the other day?" she said.
"Can't you see I'm busy?"
said Dongwa as he flipped
through the air.

"What's the matter, Sagwa?" asked Mama.

"It's no fair," said Sagwa. "Sheegwa and Dongwa are such good acrobats, but I can't even do one silly somersault."

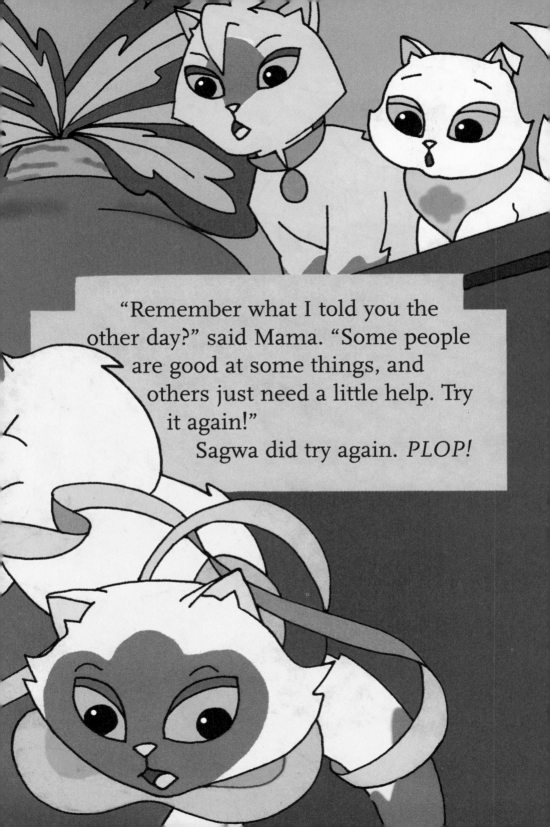

"Remember what I told you the other day?" said Mama. "Some people are good at some things, and others just need a little help. Try it again!"

Sagwa did try again. *PLOP!*

"Gee, Sagwa," said Dongwa. "You might as well give up. You'll *never* do a somersault."

"Yeah, Sagwa," added Sheegwa. "Never!"

Sagwa ran into the garden and climbed a tree. She wanted to be alone.

"Hey, watch where you're going!"
It was her best friend, Fu-Fu.
"Sorry, Fu-Fu," said Sagwa. "I didn't
see you hanging there."
"Why do you look
so sad?" asked Fu-Fu.

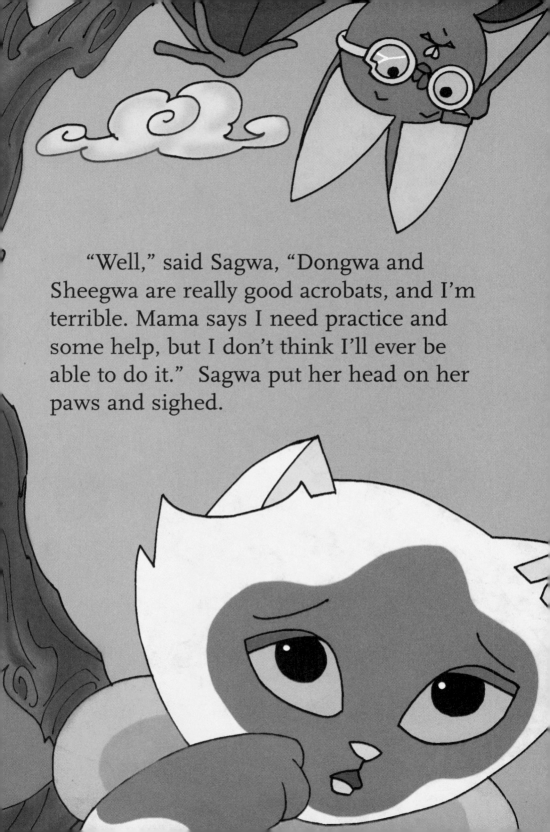

"Well," said Sagwa, "Dongwa and Sheegwa are really good acrobats, and I'm terrible. Mama says I need practice and some help, but I don't think I'll ever be able to do it." Sagwa put her head on her paws and sighed.

"Try to think about all the things that you *are* good at," said Fu-Fu. "Like writing and drawing. And being a good friend!"

"Thanks, Fu-Fu," said Sagwa. She thought for a moment. "But I *still* want to fly through the air like an acrobat!"

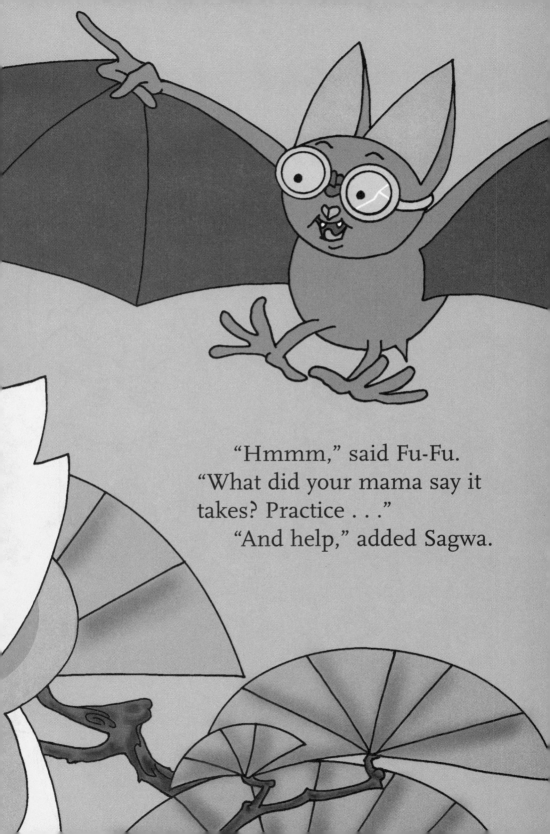

"Hmmm," said Fu-Fu.
"What did your mama say it
takes? Practice . . ."
"And help," added Sagwa.

Later that day, Mama and Baba were watching as Dongwa and Sheegwa did one somersault after another. All of a sudden, they heard laughter coming toward them.

Her family looked up and saw Sagwa flying through the air with Fu-Fu's help. Fu-Fu was flapping his wings as hard as he could and holding on to Sagwa's collar.

"Wheee! This is fun!" called Sagwa.

Then Sagwa did a beautiful flip
and landed without a *PLOP!*
"See," said Mama
proudly, "what did I tell
you? All it takes is
practice."

"Well, I did have some help," said Sagwa, smiling at Fu-Fu. "But I finally got to fly through the air like an acrobat!"

She turned and headed toward the palace. "Where are you going?" asked Dongwa. "Do it again! That was cool!"

"I don't have time," said Sagwa. "Some people are good at some things, and some people are good at others. I'm good at calligraphy, but I won't be if I don't practice."

"Hey, Sagwa – need a lift?" asked Fu-Fu, grabbing her collar and flying toward the palace. "Wheeeee!!!!" cried Sagwa. "See . . . all it takes is practice, and help from a friend!"

GLOSSARY

Dongwa:
winter melon, also
called honeydew melon.

Fu-Fu: lucky bat.

Acrobat:
someone who can do tricks like
somersaults or walking on a tightrope.

Calligraphy:
a type of special handwriting.

Courage

Scroll:
a roll of paper or parchment
used for writing.

Somersault:
to leap or roll in a circle so that
the feet go over the head.